MAY   2017

Fay Loves Ballet

Mary Elizabeth Salzmann

Consulting Editor, Diane Craig, M.A./Reading Specialist

ABDO
Publishing Company

Published by ABDO Publishing Company, 4940 Viking Drive, Edina, Minnesota 55435.

Printed in the United States.

Credits
Edited by: Pam Price
Curriculum Coordinator: Nancy Tuminelly
Cover and Interior Design and Production: Mighty Media
Photo and Illustration Credits: BananaStock Ltd., Brand X Pictures, Comstock, Corbis Images, Digital Vision, Eyewire Images, Hemera, Tracy Kompelien, PhotoDisc

Library of Congress Cataloging-in-Publication Data

Salzmann, Mary Elizabeth, 1968-
     Fay loves ballet / Mary Elizabeth Salzmann.
        p. cm. -- (Rhyme time)
     Includes index.
     ISBN 1-59197-790-8 (hardcover)
     ISBN 1-59197-896-3 (paperback)
     1. English language--Rhyme--Juvenile literature. I. Title. II. Rhyme time (ABDO Publishing Company)

     PE1517.S353 2004
     428.1'3--dc22

                                                                                    2004049516

SandCastle™ books are created by a professional team of educators, reading specialists, and content developers around five essential components that include phonemic awareness, phonics, vocabulary, text comprehension, and fluency. All books are written, reviewed, and leveled for guided reading, early intervention reading, and Accelerated Reader® programs and designed for use in shared, guided, and independent reading and writing activities to support a balanced approach to literacy instruction.

Let Us Know

After reading the book, SandCastle would like you to tell us your stories about reading. What is your favorite page? Was there something hard that you needed help with? Share the ups and downs of learning to read. We want to hear from you! To get posted on the ABDO Publishing Company Web site, send us e-mail at:

sandcastle@abdopub.com

SandCastle Level: Fluent

Words that rhyme do
not have to be spelled the
same. These words rhyme
with each other:

ballet

play

bouquet

sleigh

day

stay

obey

tray

pay

weigh

Dee Dee and Briana are best friends.

They see each other every day.

Audrey gets to dance in a ballet.

Margaret and her parents are finished shopping.

They go to a cashier to pay.

Jonathan has a yellow and white **bouquet**.

Soccer is Antonio's favorite sport to play.

Kathryn has a dog named Bongo.

She teaches him to obey.

It is time to go home.

But Jade and Leonard wish they could **stay** at the beach longer.

Marissa and her family go for a ride in a **sleigh**.

Sleigh Rides
555-1515

Kenneth carries breakfast on a tray.

Lindsey and Sabrina put things on the scale to see how much they **weigh**.

Fay Loves Ballet

Fay loved to watch the ballet.

It's all she wanted to do, day after day.

Her mother asked, "Fay,
why don't you go out and play?"

But Fay did not obey.

She just sat and watched ballet.

Then she heard a noise
that would not go away.

She looked out the window
and saw a stray.

She let him in and asked,
"Mom, can he stay?"

Her mother said, "Yes, Fay.

But you'll have to take care of him
and watch less ballet."

Fay said, "Okay!"
and named the stray Ray.

Then she went back to watching ballet.

The next thing she knew,
the little stray, Ray,
had jumped up on the table
and knocked over a bouquet!

Then he spun around
and landed on a tray!

Fay said, "Wow! It's like Ray
is trying to dance a ballet!"

She stopped watching ballet
and danced with Ray the stray.

Rhyming Riddle

What do you call a lost sled?

Stray sleigh

Glossary

ballet. a performance in which dance, costumes, and scenery are used to tell a story

bouquet. a bunch of flowers gathered together or arranged in a vase

obey. to follow rules, orders, or directions

sleigh. an open vehicle, usually pulled by horses, with runners for travel on ice or snow

stray. a pet that is wandering around or lost; having wandered or escaped from its proper or intended location

About SandCastle™

A professional team of educators, reading specialists, and content developers created the SandCastle™ series to support young readers as they develop reading skills and strategies and increase their general knowledge. The SandCastle™ series has four levels that correspond to early literacy development in young children. The levels are provided to help teachers and parents select the appropriate books for young readers.

Emerging Readers
(no flags)

Beginning Readers
(1 flag)

Transitional Readers
(2 flags)

Fluent Readers
(3 flags)

These levels are meant only as a guide. All levels are subject to change.

To see a complete list of SandCastle™ books and other nonfiction titles from ABDO Publishing Company, visit www.abdopub.com or contact us at:
4940 Viking Drive, Edina, Minnesota 55435 • 1-800-800-1312 • fax: 1-952-831-1632